The Adventures of Sophie Bean

The Red Flyer Roller Coaster

written by
Kathryn Yevchak

illustrated by
Judith Pfeiffer

KAEDEN BOOKS

Title: The Adventures of Sophie Bean, The Red Flyer Roller Coaster
Copyright © 2007 Kaeden Corporation
Author: Kathryn Yevchak
Illustrator: Judith Pfeiffer

ISBN: 978-1-57874-337-7

Published by:
      Kaeden Corporation
      P.O. Box 16190
      Rocky River, Ohio 44116
      1-800-890-7323
      www.kaeden.com

Printed in Canada

10 9 8 7 6 5 4 3 2

Contents

—1—

Still Not Tall Enough

"TOO SMALL!" announced Measuring Man.

"Are you sure I'm not tall enough?" pleaded Sophie Bean.

"Sorry, you must be 44 inches tall to ride the Red Flyer Roller Coaster. You are only 43 inches," answered Measuring Man, as he guarded the entrance to the roller coaster with his tall measuring stick.

"NEXT!" he called to Sophie Bean's twin cousins, Ryan and Parker.

"Sophie Bean, Sophie Bean, the littlest bean we've ever seen!" sung Ryan and Parker.

"Another summer and you're still not tall enough!" said Ryan.

"Forty-six inches!" announced Measuring Man to Parker. "Forty-seven inches! Enjoy the ride," he said to Ryan.

Sophie Bean turned and slowly walked back down the stairs of the roller coaster toward Mommy and Aunt Lynn.

"I'm so tired of sitting and watching them. I wanted to go on the Red Flyer this year," said Sophie Bean.

Every Friday night during the summer, Mommy and Aunt Lynn brought the three cousins to the amusement park on the boardwalk to ride their favorite rides. It was only a few miles from where they all lived.

The Red Flyer was Ryan and Parker's favorite ride because it was the tallest roller coaster in the park. The Red Flyer was also Sophie Bean's favorite, but she was still too small to ride it.

Sophie Bean saw Ryan and Parker

waving their hands in the air as the Red Flyer slowly climbed the first big hill.

"I want to see the view from that hill," said Sophie Bean.

Click, click, click . . . the roller coaster climbed and climbed the big hill. Sophie Bean saw Ryan and Parker looking around.

Each numbered car on the Red

Flyer was red with a different color dragon on its side. "Look, they're in Parker's favorite car," said Sophie Bean, pointing up toward them. Parker's favorite car was the Number 5 Car with the green dragon.

The roller coaster finally reached the top of the hill. Suddenly, it took off down the hill going faster and faster. Sophie Bean saw Ryan and Parker laughing as the Red Flyer zoomed around.

"I don't know if I can watch this every week again," said Sophie Bean. She just had to get on that roller coaster.

—2—

No More Baby Rides

When they got home, Sophie Bean called her Grandma on the phone. "Grandma, I'm still not tall enough to go on the Red Flyer."

"Aren't there plenty of other rides?" asked Grandma. "You used to love the merry-go-round."

"The merry-go-round is for babies, Grandma! I'm too big for that now. I want to ride the Red Flyer and it's always the same—Ryan and Parker get to go on and I have to watch them."

"Do you remember when you were too small to reach the pedals on the bicycle I bought you for your birthday? You had to keep riding your tricycle for a while. Now look at you—you can ride that bicycle all over the place," said Grandma.

Sophie Bean hung up with Grandma feeling a little bit better, but not really. She still didn't want to wait for another summer to ride the Red Flyer.

—3—

Ryan's High Heels?

The next week, Mommy called through the house, "Sophie Bean! The amusement park opens in ten minutes. Everyone is waiting for you in the car."

Sophie Bean waited in her bedroom until she heard Mommy go outside. Then she grabbed her purple backpack and quickly ran down the steps, slamming the front door behind her. She climbed into her usual seat between Ryan and Parker in the backseat of Aunt Lynn's car.

SOPHIE BEAN

13

"What are you doing with your backpack?" asked Parker.

"It's none of your business, Parker!" said Sophie Bean as she tried to hide the backpack under the front seat. Parker reached down to grab it.

"Parker, leave it alone!" cried Sophie Bean.

Parker was too quick. He grabbed the backpack and handed it over to Ryan. Ryan quickly unzipped it to see what was inside.

Out of the backpack Ryan pulled a pair of Mommy's bright red, high-heeled, strappy sandals.

"Ryan, what in the world are you doing with those?" asked Mommy, as she turned around to see what all the noise was in the backseat.

"They're not mine! I found them in Sophie Bean's backpack," said Ryan.

"I just have to be tall enough for the Red Flyer!" said Sophie Bean, as she started to cry.

"Nice try, Sophie Bean, but you might fall and hurt yourself if you try walking in those. Hand them over, Ryan," said Mommy.

"Sophie Bean, Sophie Bean, the littlest bean we've ever seen!" sang the boys.

Sophie Bean crossed her arms with a sigh and stared out the car window.

—4—

Sudsy Sophie

The next week, Mommy and Aunt Lynn were busy packing for a day trip to the beach. Sophie Bean found Mommy by the car and announced, "I can't go. My legs hurt."

"What are you talking about, Sophie Bean?" asked Mommy.

"I said I can't go. My legs hurt."

Mommy looked Sophie Bean's legs up and down. "Let me see you walk," she said.

Sophie Bean walked across the yard.

"Your legs are fine, Sophie Bean. Can you help me get these beach toys into the car?" asked Mommy.

At the beach, Mommy and Aunt Lynn sat near the lifeguard. By the time they finished lunch, Sophie Bean had forgotten all about her aching legs.

"Remember, no swimming for an hour after lunch," said Aunt Lynn.

"Let's go over to the playground," said Ryan.

They ran over to the beach playground. Climbing on the jungle gym next to Sophie Bean was a little boy.

"Hi, my name is Sophie Bean."

"Hi, Soapie! My name is Max."

"Not Soapie–Sophie!" But the little boy had already walked away toward the slide.

Parker pretended to wash his hair as he came up with a new rhyme: "Soapie Bean, Soapie Bean, the cleanest bean I've ever seen!"

—5—

Curlers, Curlers Everywhere

A few weeks later, as everyone got ready to leave for the amusement park, Mommy asked, "Have you seen Sophie Bean? It's almost time to go."

"She's still in the bathroom getting ready. Girls are so weird!" Parker rolled his eyes.

"Sophie Bean, are you okay in there?" Mommy asked as she knocked on the bathroom door.

Out came Sophie Bean with her blonde hair piled high on her head in

Mommy's pink, fuzzy curlers. "Now I'm tall enough for the Red Flyer!" announced Sophie Bean.

Ryan and Parker fell on the floor laughing. "Sophie Bean, your hair doesn't count toward the 44 inches," said Parker.

"It's time to go," said Aunt Lynn.

It took Sophie Bean a long time to walk to Aunt Lynn's car because she was trying to hold her head very still so that none of the curlers would fall out. She lowered herself onto her usual seat. Ryan and Parker kept poking her shoulder trying to get her to look at them, but Sophie Bean didn't budge. The only time she moved was after each big bump the car hit on the road. She would reach her hand up to make sure the curlers were still safely in place.

Ryan and Parker could barely stand how long it took to walk to the Red Flyer—they had to wait for Sophie Bean, who was walking so slowly because of the curlers. She knew this was her big chance to get on the Red Flyer.

When they finally reached the Red Flyer, Sophie Bean carefully climbed the steps to the entrance where Measuring Man stood. Ryan and Parker were behind her and nearly bumping into her. "Hurry up, Sophie Bean!" said Ryan.

When she finally reached Measuring Man and he held up the measuring stick, it was all Sophie Bean could do to stay still long enough to keep the curlers in place. She was almost on the Red Flyer.

"Okay, you're 44 inches." Measuring Man waved her onto the ride. Ryan and Parker were speechless. Sophie Bean quickly turned to get on the roller coaster. She was going on the Red Flyer!

But then, just as Measuring Man was about to look away from Sophie Bean, he saw something on the top of her head. Suddenly, one of the curlers from the very top of her head fell off! Now one side of Sophie Bean's head was taller than the other.

"Wait a minute . . . " said Measuring Man as he looked from one side of Sophie Bean to the other. "I thought you were tall enough, but it was just your hair in the curlers. TOO SMALL!"

Sophie Bean's shoulders sank.

Ryan and Parker gave each other high fives as they danced their way past Sophie Bean onto the roller coaster. "Sophie Bean, Sophie Bean, the littlest bean we've ever seen!" they sang.

Sophie Bean's eyes filled with tears as she turned and ran down the stairs with curlers flying off her head in every direction. "I don't know how much more of this I can take," she cried.

—6—

Too Small . . . Again!

Every week it was the same thing. Friday night would arrive and Sophie Bean would raise her head as high as she could, stretching her neck as far as it would go and wait for Measuring Man's decision. "TOO SMALL," Measuring Man would announce and Ryan and Parker would sing, "Sophie Bean, Sophie Bean, the littlest bean we've ever seen!"

"Sophie Bean, even if you were tall enough to go on the Red Flyer, you'd probably cry! Remember last year when Cousin Connor took you on the Ferris wheel for the first time? You cried so loud that they had to stop the ride so you could get off," laughed Ryan.

"You just wait, Ryan, someday I'll be tall enough," said Sophie Bean.

—7—

Oh, Those Aching Legs

Finally, it was time for a visit from Grandma.

"Grandma, I'm still not tall enough to ride the Red Flyer. Ryan and Parker won't stop teasing me about it."

"When I was little, your Uncle Stan used to laugh at me all the time for being shorter than him. Now look at us—he's so short that I can see the top of his bald head!" laughed Grandma.

That night, Sophie Bean woke up with aching legs again. She decided to get a glass of water. On her way to the kitchen, she saw Grandma watching television.

"Sophie Bean, is everything alright?"

"Grandma, I can't sleep because my legs won't stop aching," said Sophie Bean.

"That sounds like growing pains to me," answered Grandma. "Your legs are growing so fast that it hurts. I bet it won't be long before you are riding the Red Flyer."

Grandma shuffled Sophie Bean back into bed and rubbed her legs until she fell asleep.

—8—

One Last Chance for Air Time

With Grandma's visit, there was so much to do: swimming in the ocean, building sandcastles on the beach, eating ice cream cones on the boardwalk, and watching fireworks.

One day Aunt Lynn announced, "Guess what? It's almost the end of the summer. This week will be our last trip to the amusement park."

That Friday night, Sophie Bean walked straight to the bench to sit and watch Ryan and Parker go on the Red Flyer for the last time that summer.

"What's the matter, Sophie Bean? Don't you want to hear 'TOO SMALL' one more time?" asked Parker.

"I don't have to go if I don't want to," said Sophie Bean.

"Come on, Sophie Bean—Measuring Man is waiting," said Ryan.

"Fine!" she announced. Sophie Bean marched up to Measuring Man and awaited his decision. She didn't even bother stretching her neck or getting on her tippy toes.

Measuring Man held his measuring stick up to Sophie Bean. "Go ahead," he said.

"What did you say?" asked Sophie Bean.

"Go ahead. You're tall enough," repeated Measuring Man. "Enjoy the ride. NEXT!"

Ryan and Parker could not believe it. "No! It can't be! She's too small to go on with us! Measure her again," Parker said.

Holding up the measuring stick again, Measuring Man pointed, "See, she's tall enough."

A huge grin spread across Sophie Bean's face.

"They were growing pains!" she exclaimed.

Sophie Bean started to walk toward the entrance to the roller coaster and then she froze. She saw the Red Flyer's enormous first hill. It looked a lot higher than she remembered. Sophie Bean saw Ryan and Parker looking at her and she heard the song in her head again, "Sophie Bean, Sophie Bean, the littlest bean we've ever seen!"

"I'm going on!" she decided. Sophie Bean ran toward the Number 3 Car with the purple dragon on it. But then suddenly she stopped in her tracks, "Oh, no! I'm going to have to ride alone!" Each car only held two people.

She looked around quickly for Ryan and Parker. They were already buckled into their seats in Ryan's favorite, the Number 10 Car with the blue dragon on it. She thought of turning around and running back to Mommy but she didn't want to lose her spot on the Number 3 Car. She didn't know what to do.

Suddenly, from behind her she heard, "Don't worry, Sophie Bean, I'll go on with you." It was Grandma!

"Grandma, you're the best!" said Sophie Bean.

"Let's rock and roll!" shouted Grandma.

Sophie Bean climbed into the car, buckled her seatbelt and was ready to go. She couldn't stop smiling as the ride began.

Click, click, click . . . the Red Flyer
began the slow climb up its tallest
peak. Sophie Bean looked over the
side and saw Mommy and Aunt Lynn
growing smaller in the distance.

She was afraid to let go and wave
to them. Her heart was beating so
fast! She wasn't sure that the roller
coaster would ever reach the top of
the hill. Could it go any higher?

"Look, Sophie Bean, we can see the entire park," said Grandma. It was true—Sophie Bean could see the entire park, the whole beach and far out over the ocean.

Finally, the roller coaster made its way over the top of the hill and then they were off! Zooming along the track, Sophie Bean felt the wind blowing through her hair. She closed her eyes for a few seconds but opened them again because she didn't want to miss anything. As they sped over the next hill, Sophie Bean felt her whole body lift up out of the seat just a little bit.

"Air time!" shouted Parker. Sophie Bean held on a little more tightly. Up and down, twist and dive, over and under . . . ZOOM! Around and around the Red Flyer went.

"Is it over already?" asked Sophie Bean as they pulled to a stop. They were all laughing and giggling with excitement.

"Mommy, I had so much fun!" shouted Sophie Bean as she ran off the roller coaster. "I want to go on again," she said looking at Grandma.

"One ride is enough for an old lady like me. Ryan, Parker, one of you go with Sophie Bean," ordered Grandma.

"I'll go," offered Ryan.

Over and over, Ryan and Parker took turns riding the Red Flyer with Sophie Bean. Then, Measuring Man announced, "Last ride!"

Sophie Bean looked around. "Parker, will you go on with me one more time?"

"No, Sophie Bean, it's time to go get ice cream," he whined.

Ryan agreed, "It's ice cream time."

"Not until I go on one more time!" said Sophie Bean.

Sophie Bean waved her arms in the night air as she rode the Red Flyer alone on its last turn around the tracks for the summer.

Afterwards, Sophie Bean couldn't stop smiling as she ate her ice cream cone. She felt very tall and very proud. She even came up with her own rhyme that she sang loudly to Ryan and Parker, "Sophie Bean, Sophie Bean, the BRAVEST bean you've ever seen!"